MINDFULNESS

WELLNESS
MIND BODY MOTION

Sheelagh Matthews

www.openlightbox.com

Step 1
Go to **www.openlightbox.com**

Step 2
Enter this unique code
YUDCMKDNT

Step 3
Explore your interactive eBook!

AV2 is optimized for use on any device

Your interactive eBook comes with...

Contents
Browse a live contents page to easily navigate through resources

Audio
Listen to sections of the book read aloud

Videos
Watch informative video clips

Weblinks
Gain additional information for research

Slideshows
View images and captions

Try This!
Complete activities and hands-on experiments

Key Words
Study vocabulary, and complete a matching word activity

Quizzes
Test your knowledge

Share
Share titles within your Learning Management System (LMS) or Library Circulation System

Citation
Create bibliographical references following the Chicago Manual of Style

This title is part of our AV2 digital subscription

1-Year 3–8 Subscription
ISBN 978-1-7911-3306-1

Access hundreds of AV2 titles with our digital subscription.
Sign up for a FREE trial at **www.openlightbox.com/trial**

MINDFULNESS

What Is Mindfulness?

Mindfulness is a simple yet powerful ancient wellness **practice**. It involves paying full attention to one's thoughts, feelings, senses, and surroundings. A kind, non-judging attitude is also important. People reach a mindful state by slowing down and focusing on their breathing.

Being mindful is about learning to be in the moment. It takes only a few minutes to be mindful. This can be done at any time in any place. Anyone can practice mindfulness, no matter their age, religion, or **culture**.

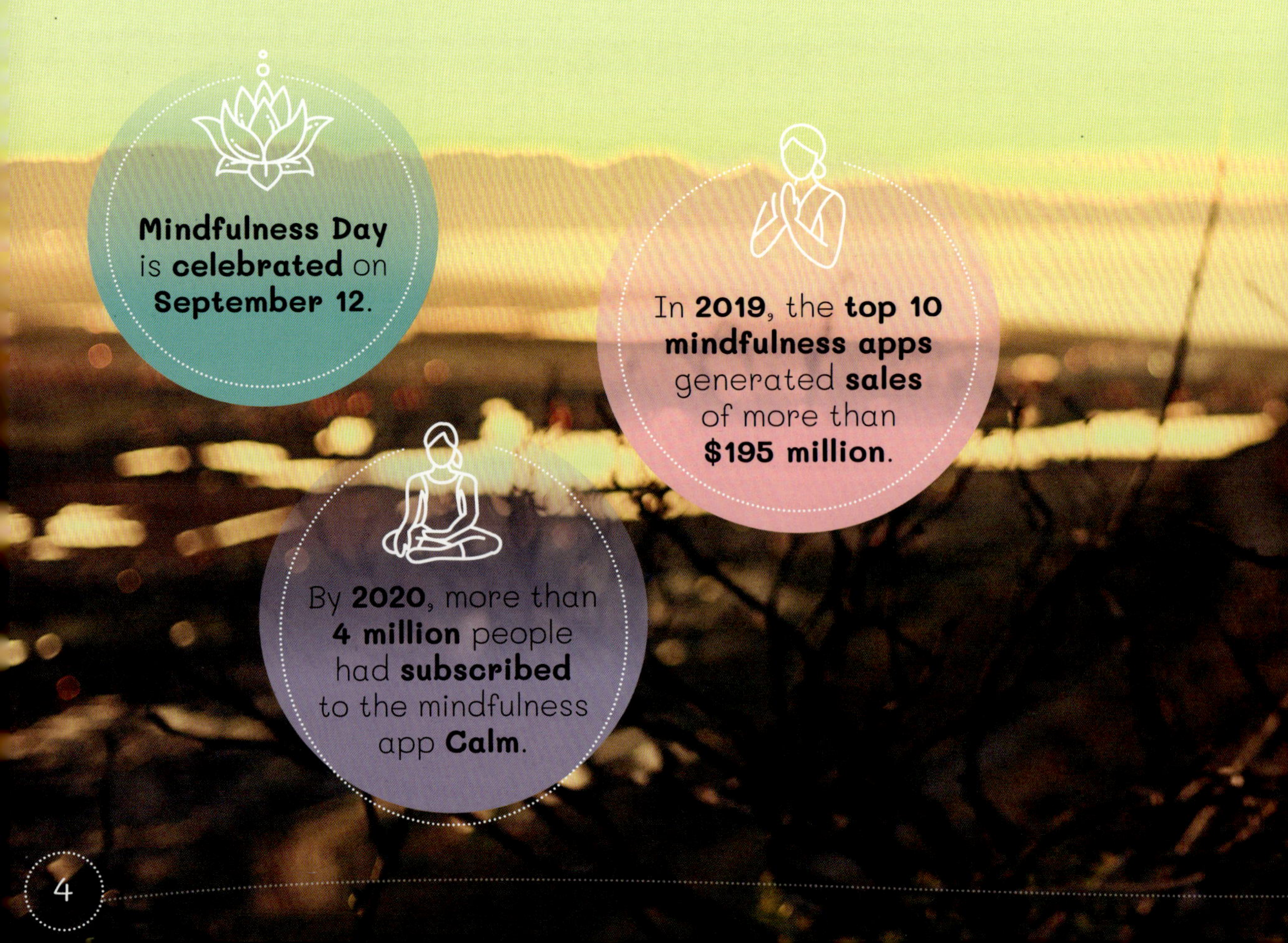

Mindfulness Day is **celebrated** on **September 12**.

In **2019**, the **top 10 mindfulness apps** generated **sales** of more than **$195 million**.

By **2020**, more than **4 million** people had **subscribed** to the mindfulness app **Calm**.

Mindfulness is good for both the mind and the body. It can help people reduce fear and **stress**. Mindfulness allows people to relax, boosts health, and improves focus as well. It can also help people understand themselves better.

How It Started

Mindfulness was first practiced about 2,500 years ago. It is believed to have its roots in **Buddhism**. For a long time, Buddhism was practiced only in Asian countries. It was brought to the **West** by immigrants in the mid-1800s.

A **monk** named Thich Nhat Hanh is credited with bringing Buddhist-style mindfulness to the West. He came from Vietnam to the United States in the 1960s to teach religion to university students. Later, he founded a community in France. It was known as Plum Village. Today, people from all over the world go there to learn how to live their lives in a mindful way. Thich Nhat Hanh has also written several books on mindfulness.

Thich Nhat Hanh

One of the people who studied under Thich Nhat Hanh was Jon Kabat-Zinn. In 1979, he founded the Mindfulness-Based Stress Reduction program at the University of Massachusetts. Although based on Buddhist mindfulness, Kabat-Zinn's program was not religious. His training included how to be non-judgmental and present in the moment. Mindfulness programs have continued to grow in the West ever since.

Timeline

2,500 years ago Buddhist monks in Asia begin the practice of mindfulness.

Mid-1800s Asian immigrants bring Buddhism to the West.

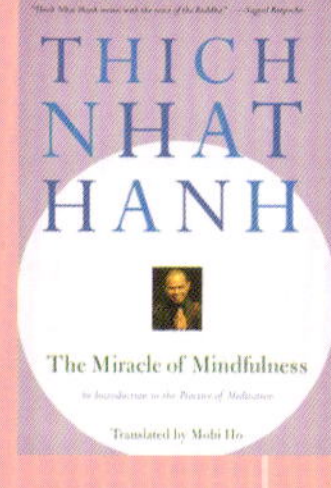

1975 *The Miracle of Mindfulness*, by Thich Nhat Hanh, is published.

1979 Jon Kabat-Zinn creates the Mindfulness-Based Stress Reduction program at the University of Massachusetts.

2000s Mindfulness programs begin to appear in schools and workplaces.

2021 Research shows that online mindfulness practices may reduce fear, anxiety, and stress during the **COVID-19 pandemic.**

Ready for Mindfulness

Mindfulness does not require any special clothing or equipment. It only needs a person's focused attention and some time set aside.

A casual mindfulness session might take just one or two minutes. It typically involves only the participant. A **meditation** session with a teacher might last 10 minutes or longer.

Support

Before starting a mindfulness session, it is important to create an environment that feels safe and comfortable. Clothing, company, and personal items can all work to make a mindfulness experience more meaningful.

Clothing

A person should wear something that makes them feel comfortable. This will allow the person to relax and focus on being mindful. Some people may prefer a loose top and pants. Others might wear a stretchy yoga outfit.

Space

Mindfulness is best achieved in a quiet space. Possible places for a session may include a bedroom or under a favorite tree. A **dedicated** place for mindfulness lets the brain know it will soon be entering a mindful state.

Cushion and Blanket

Cushions and blankets are useful during a mindfulness session. A blanket can make lying on the floor more comfortable. It can also be used as a cover if warmth is needed. A cushion can be used to sit on or to support the back.

A Trusted Friend

Exploring emotions is a mindful thing to do. Some people may want to talk after a mindfulness session. Sharing thoughts and feelings with a trusted **confidant** can add depth to a mindfulness experience. This person can be a parent, teacher, or friend.

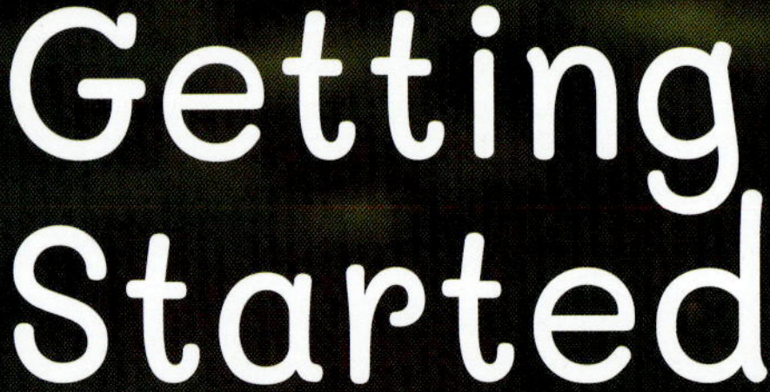

Getting Started

One of the first steps of a mindfulness warmup is to prepare mentally for the session to come. This is often an internal conversation people have with themselves. It acknowledges that time is going to be set aside for mindfulness. People can then begin to focus on entering a calm state.

Establishing a comfortable space is important to this process. How this is done will be unique to each individual. A person may go to a favorite room, sit in a soft chair, or lie on the floor with a blanket. In a group session, the teacher may provide tools or exercises to help in this area as well.

Once the person has settled into the space, breathing exercises can help deepen relaxation. Teachers often encourage their students to close their eyes and take a few deep breaths. The students are told to focus on how each breath feels. This is a time to empty the mind of outside problems and focus on the here and now. Once this is done, the mindfulness session can begin.

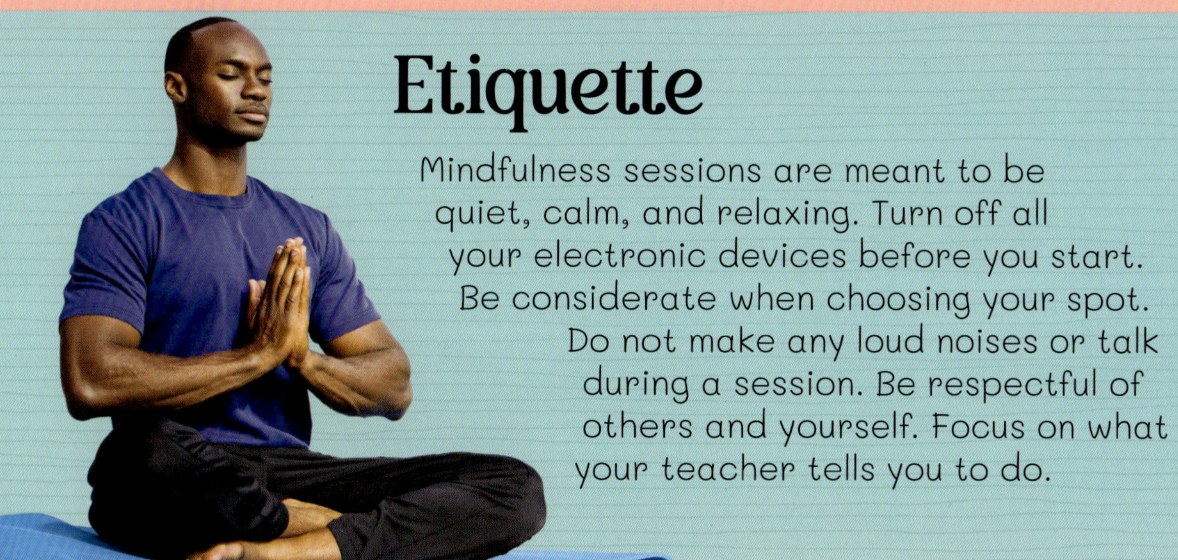

Etiquette

Mindfulness sessions are meant to be quiet, calm, and relaxing. Turn off all your electronic devices before you start. Be considerate when choosing your spot. Do not make any loud noises or talk during a session. Be respectful of others and yourself. Focus on what your teacher tells you to do.

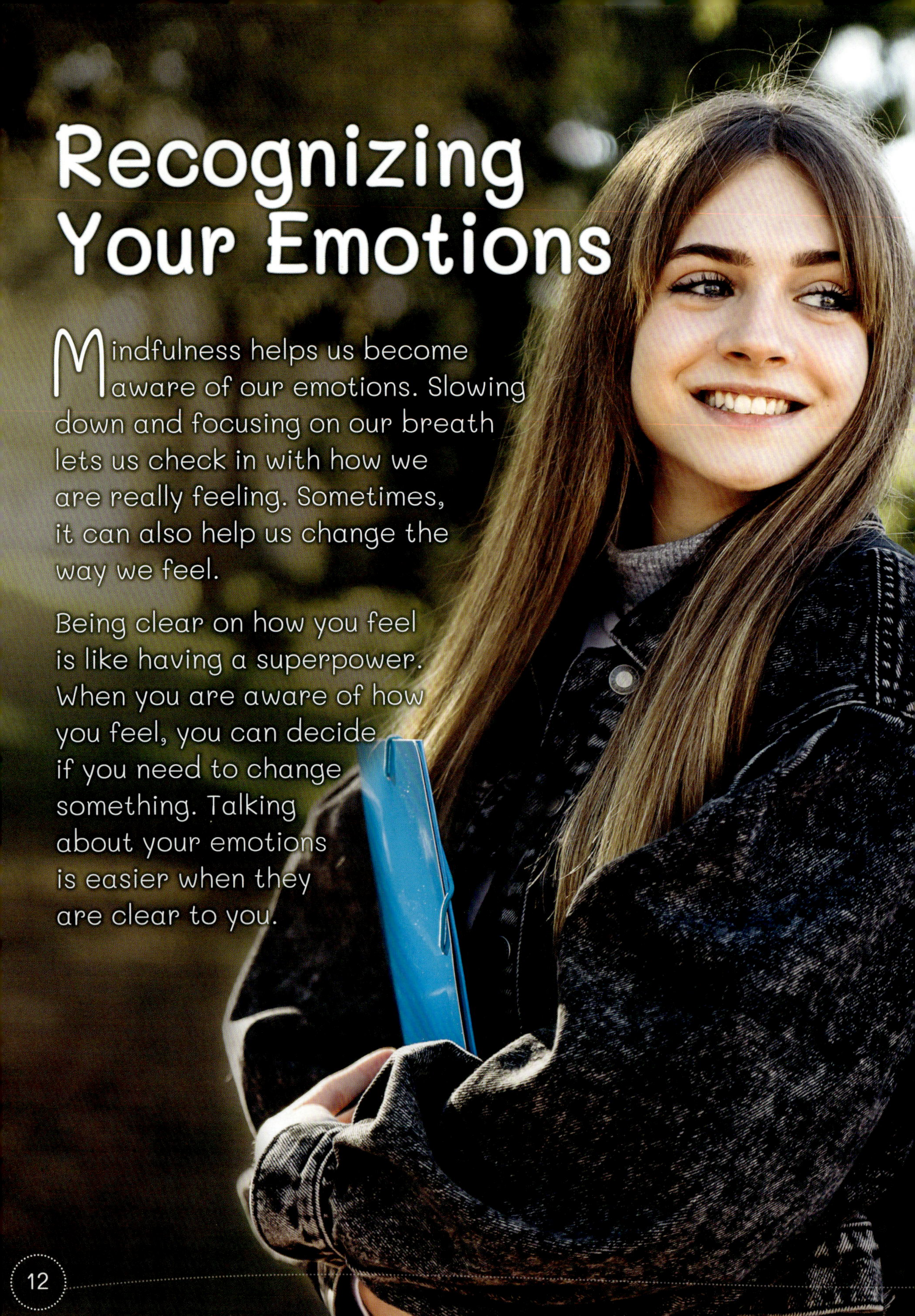

Recognizing Your Emotions

Mindfulness helps us become aware of our emotions. Slowing down and focusing on our breath lets us check in with how we are really feeling. Sometimes, it can also help us change the way we feel.

Being clear on how you feel is like having a superpower. When you are aware of how you feel, you can decide if you need to change something. Talking about your emotions is easier when they are clear to you.

Which Face Are You?

Before starting a mindfulness session, check in with yourself. Look at the chart below. Choose the face that best matches how you are feeling. Rank your feeling from 1 to 10.

After your session, revisit the chart and repeat the activity. See if your feelings have changed at all. You may feel entirely different or a little better than you did before.

In The Moment

The transition from the warmup to the mindfulness session should be seamless. There should be no interruption between the two stages. It is important for people to stay fully in the moment and remain focused. This will ensure that they reach a mindful state.

To learn how to maintain this flow, people new to mindfulness usually take guided meditations led by a teacher. These are often found online. As they are guided, the meditations have established steps. The teacher provides students with specific things to focus on. These may include a sound, a visual, or simply the breath. By following the teacher's lead, students stay focused and in the present moment.

Some teachers add affirmations to their guided meditations. Affirmations are positive statements people say to themselves. These include, "I can do this," or "It is okay to be myself." The statements work to build **confidence** and bring positive thoughts to life. Students may be asked to say them quietly or to silently think them. The affirmations may be repeated throughout the session.

As people become more comfortable with mindfulness meditation, they may decide to do it alone. Some may follow the format of their guided sessions. Others will adapt the meditations to meet their own needs.

Approximately **40 percent** of all Americans say they **meditate** at least **once per week**.

More than **2,500 mindfulness apps** have been launched since 2015.

The most **live views** of a meditation on YouTube was **58,162**, in 2021.

Get to Know Yourself

You can practice mindfulness in many ways. Each can help you to connect with yourself and your present world. Some methods require stillness. Others are more active. Try these exercises and see how they make you feel.

Leaves on a Stream

This exercise will help you pay attention to your thoughts in a non-judging way.

1. Sit down in a place that feels comfortable. Close your eyes.
2. Imagine that you are sitting beside a gently flowing stream that has leaves floating along its surface. Spend a few seconds watching the leaves.
3. As thoughts enter your mind, take each one, whether positive or negative, and place it on a leaf. Watch each leaf float away.
4. If your thoughts come to a stop, continue to watch the stream and wait for more. When they start again, continue placing them on the leaves and watching them float by. Let the thoughts come to you at their own pace. Do not rush them.
5. Continue the activity for a few more minutes. Then, slowly draw your focus away from the stream and back to where you are. When you are ready, open your eyes to end the activity.

Tense and Release

Performing this exercise will help you become aware of your body and how it is feeling in the here and now.

1. Lie down in a comfortable spot. Close your eyes. Take a few deep breaths.
2. Squeeze the muscles in your feet as tightly as you can. Make sure to curl your toes so that they are squeezed as well.
3. After a few seconds, release all of the muscles you have tensed. Let your feet relax.

4. Continue to work your way up your body. Tense and relax your legs, stomach, chest, arms, and neck, one at a time. As you squeeze each body part, think about how it feels.
5. When you have squeezed all your body parts, take a finishing breath. Then, open your eyes. Give yourself time to feel the space around you.

Heartbeat Exercise

This activity helps you to focus on yourself in the present moment.

1. Begin by jumping up and down 10 times.
2. When you are done, sit down. Put your hand over your heart.
3. Close your eyes. Focus on your breath and the beat of your heart. Think about how both feel.
4. Once your heartbeat returns to normal, open your eyes. Let yourself become aware of your surroundings again.

Checking In

Guided meditation usually ends on a gentle note. People might be asked to notice how their bodies feel, and then to slowly open their eyes. These same steps can be taken when people practice mindfulness on their own.

It is important that people continue to check in with themselves throughout the day. Checking in develops self-awareness. It uncovers what people can do on their own to make their lives better. The goal of checking in is for people to find out how they feel and to plan future actions.

One way people can start to check in is to identify the emotions they are experiencing. This can lead them to explore these emotions further. If people like how they feel, they can determine what they like about it. If they do not like the feeling, they can ask themselves what they do not like.

These questions can help people take even more steps to feel better about themselves. They may write about their emotions in a journal. They might decide to go for a walk. Some people may decide they need to talk to another person about their feelings. In doing so, these people are practicing mindfulness.

The Benefits of Mindfulness

Practicing mindfulness can benefit the mind, body, and spirit. Its focus on the present allows people to savor life as it happens and let go of things they cannot control. As a result, people who practice mindfulness are better able to relax. They are less prone to fear, anxiety, and stress.

Relationships benefit from mindfulness as well. People who practice mindfulness have been proven to listen more and get along well with others. They are better able to control their emotions.

Mindfulness has been shown to improve a person's mental functions. Its meditative qualities work to improve memory and focus. It also helps to tune out distractions.

About **89 percent of students** who meditate and practice mindfulness have **improved control of their emotions**.

Meditating just **10 minutes each day** can curb **unhealthy food cravings** by about **40 percent**.

More than **75 percent** of people who **meditate** do so for its **general wellness benefits**.

Being mindful has physical benefits as well. It boosts the **immune system**, which helps to fight off illness. It also improves a person's sleep. Mindfulness practices have been used to treat health problems such as high blood pressure and heart disease.

Mindfulness Quiz

1. Who is credited with bringing Buddhist-style mindfulness to the West?
2. Who founded the Mindfulness-Based Stress Reduction program at the University of Massachusetts?
3. What are affirmations?
4. Which mindfulness resources are often found online?
5. When is Mindfulness Day?
6. How long does a meditation session with a teacher usually last?
7. What percentage of people who meditate do it for its general wellness benefits?
8. Which health problems have mindfulness practices been used to treat?
9. How many mindfulness apps have been launched since 2015?
10. For how long have people been practicing mindfulness?

ANSWERS

1. Thich Nhat Hanh **2.** Jon Kabat-Zinn **3.** Positive statements people say to themselves **4.** Guided meditations **5.** September 12 **6.** 10 minutes or longer **7.** More than 75 percent **8.** High blood pressure and heart disease **9.** More than 2,500 **10.** More than 2,500 years

Key Words

Buddhism: one of the world's most widespread religions

confidant: a person with whom personal matters are discussed

confidence: belief or trust in something

COVID-19 pandemic: an infectious disease that was discovered in 2019 and spread to countries around the world

culture: the arts, beliefs, and customs that make up a way of life for a group of people

dedicated: set aside for a specific purpose or use

immune system: the parts of the body that work to fight illness and disease

meditation: the practice of spending time in quiet thought

monk: a man who has joined a religious community and lives by a set of vows

practice: the doing of something over and over again to acquire or polish a skill

stress: mental or emotional strain

West: Europe and the Americas

Index

Get the best of both worlds.

AV2 bridges the gap between print and digital.

The expandable resources toolbar enables quick access to content including **videos**, **audio**, **activities**, **weblinks**, **slideshows**, **quizzes**, and **key words**.

Animated videos make static images come alive.

Resource icons on each page help readers to further **explore key concepts**.

Published by Lightbox Learning Inc.
276 5th Avenue, Suite 704 #917
New York, NY 10001
Website: www.openlightbox.com

Library of Congress Cataloging-in-Publication Data
Name: Matthews, Sheelagh, author.
Title: Mindfulness / Sheelagh Matthews.
Description: New York, NY : AV2, [2023] | Series: Wellness: mind body motion | Includes index. | Audience: Grades 2-3
Identifiers: LCCN 2021033634 (print) | LCCN 2021033635 (ebook) | ISBN 9781791142650 (library binding) | ISBN 9781791142667 (paperback) | ISBN 9781791142674
Subjects: LCSH: Mindfulness (Psychology)--Juvenile literature. | Mind and body--Juvenile literature.
Classification: LCC BF637.M56 M38 2022 (print) | LCC BF637.M56 (ebook) | DDC 158.1/3--dc23
LC record available at https://lccn.loc.gov/2021033634
LC ebook record available at https://lccn.loc.gov/2021033635

Printed in Guangzhou, China
1 2 3 4 5 6 7 8 9 0 25 24 23 22 21

122021
101121

Project Coordinator: Heather Kissock
Designer: Terry Paulhus

Photo Credits
Every reasonable effort has been made to trace ownership and to obtain permission to reprint copyright material. The publisher would be pleased to have any errors or omissions brought to its attention so that they may be corrected in subsequent printings. The publisher acknowledges Getty Images, Alamy, Dreamstime, and Shutterstock as its primary photo suppliers for this title.